The Karma

Bright Mills

Ukiyoto Publishing

All global publishing rights are held by

Ukiyoto Publishing

Published in 2022

Content Copyright © Bright Mills

ISBN 9789360169893

All rights reserved.

No part of this publication may be reproduced, transmitted, or stored in a retrieval system, in any form by any means, electronic, mechanical, photocopying, recording or otherwise, without the prior permission of the publisher.

The moral rights of the author have been asserted.

This is a work of fiction. Names, characters, businesses, places, events, locales, and incidents are either the products of the author's imagination or used in a fictitious manner. Any resemblance to actual persons, living or dead, or actual events is purely coincidental.

This book is sold subject to the condition that it shall not by way of trade or otherwise, be lent, resold, hired out or otherwise circulated, without the publisher's prior consent, in any form of binding or cover other than that in which it is published.

www.ukiyoto.com

CONTENTS

Jealous Murderer	1
Chapter 1	2
Chapter 2	6
Chapter 3	11
Will To Kill	16
Chapter 1	17
Chapter 2	21
Chapter 3	28
Stab In The Heart	32
Chapter 1	33
Chapter 2	39
Chapter 3	44
About the Author	51

Jealous Murderer

Chapter 1

Shelly Morgan, 15 years old live with her parents in Manchester, England. Her father Andy Morgan is a bus driver, while her mother Jessica Morgan, a sales person in the supermarket. Her elder sister Regina Morgan 18 years old, who is a drug addict, was placed in a youth center for rehabilitation. Her younger brother Jacob Morgan 12 years old was in a high school in Manchester. Shelly is a very rude and bad behaved girl and often run away from home. She can be away from home for weeks living with her boyfriend Tony Moses. Due to her bad attitude, her father took her to the youth center to join her elder sister for rehabilitation. Some weeks later, Shelly escaped from the youth center through the window to live with her boyfriend Tony.

Manchester is a large city in the North West of England, often known as the UK's second city behind London. The city has fantastic transport connections, allowing you to get to London by train in under two hours. As well as brilliant bus, train and tram connections, Manchester also has a large international airport – so handy for travelling during half-term breaks. With over 200 schools in Manchester alone (There are 10 other boroughs, all easily accessible from Manchester) this really is a great location to be a teacher. GSL Education have partnerships with schools and academies across the Greater Manchester region, making this a great base to work from. With a population of over 2.5 million, Manchester boasts a rich industrial heritage; It was the first industrialized city in the world! Also, the founder and leader of the British Suffragette movement, securing the right for women to vote was born and raised in Moss Side..... and the first computer in the world, The Manchester Baby, was made here!

Manchester also has a very famous sporting history. Along with the National Football Museum, it is home to both Manchester United and Manchester City premier league football clubs. Manchester is also extremely proud to be the home of the Team GB Cycling squad with the World Championships being recently held at the velodrome based in Sports City. If Rugby is more your thing, the AJ Bell stadium is home to both Sale Sharks and Salford Reds, with Wigan Warriors just a short train journey away. If none of the above tickles your fancy, then why not head over to the Emirates Old Trafford Cricket ground, home to the Lancashire County Cricket Team and just a 10-minute tram ride from the City Centre.

If fashion is more your style, then Boohoo and Misguided have all made Manchester their home. And with designer shops at the Trafford Centre and the Triangle and more bohemian feel to The Northern Quarter, you can shop until your hearts content. With such a large and diverse population, the social scene is a central hub for hedonism and known as The City of Pleasure. Its social scene definitely rivals that of London, only quite a bit cheaper and extremely welcoming. With cafes, bars, restaurants, theatres and music arenas you can literally experience something new every time you go out in the City.... Nearly forgot the Curry Mile in Rusholme where there are over 70 different eateries specializing in Asian cuisine. So not quite all Eccles Cakes and Lancashire Hotpots after all!

It's the most linguistically diverse city in western Europe, with up to 200 languages spoken in the city at any one time. It is estimated that half of the city's adult population is multilingual, with 4 in 10 young people speaking more than one language. Manchester's eclectic nightlife offers something for everyone, from the hipster bars of the Northern Quarter to the party palace of the Printworks. Greater Manchester has the highest number of theater seats per head of population outside of London, and covers the whole spectrum of fringe, opera, classical music and dance productions. The city boasts four professional orchestras, the only Comedy Store located outside of London, and a renowned independent cinema. There are numerous literary festivals hosted across the year, as well as critically acclaimed exhibitions from world- famous artists. Manchester is famed for being one of the best cities for nightlife in the UK. Whether you are looking for a gourmet dinner, upmarket wine bar, traditional 'real ale' pub or a place to dance the night away, Manchester has it all. It remains one of the best cities in the world to hear live music and is a major destination for touring bands. From jazz festivals and world music events to classical music and opera, the diversity of music available is hard to beat.

In the spring of 2006, two high school students Malin and Judith was walking in a wooden area, near their school. Along the river, they spotted what they thought is a dead animal in the water. Moving closer, they realized that it is a dead body. Terrified, they immediately alerted their teacher who called the police that Manchester high school has found a dead body in the Manchester River. Following that, a team of investigators including Sergeant Ted Morris, Mary Connell, John Mayor, and Sarah Donnelly, went to scene to begin investigation. At the time, Remy Adams was a forensic investigation specialist working with the police. Before he left for the crime scene, being a forensic investigator, he contacted the police to secure the parameter of the crime scene and prevent anyone from entering. He said it is important because if the public or the police should enter the crime scene, a lot of evidence can be destroyed. It was a huge crime scene of about 4,000 feet to examine.

Before they touch anything, even the victim, he had to take photographs so that if anybody touches something, he has a photograph as an evidence. His routine is to work outward from the victim. Remy uses a particular kind of method to ensure no part of the crime scene is overlooked. He saw the dead body lying in the water about 30 to 40 meters away from him. She was caught on the rocks, the current must have carried her to that point or the crime may have occurred there. He saw a person for sure, with a very long hair, but he could not determine if the dead body was a male or female, who was fully clothed, and dressed appropriately for the weather. It was until he got closer to the victim, turned the body he realized it was a teenager. Physically, her hands appeared normal. Her body was okay and was not very decomposed. Her body was not in an advanced state of decomposition.

The water was quite cold, about 5 degree Celsius, which help to pressure the condition of the body. Whether it was there for 24 hours, or 48 hours, or 72 hours, we still could not determine at that time, Remy stated. Are the police dealing with a crime or an accident? There was no evidence that the victim was sexually assaulted. She was fully clothed, her underwear and pant was not removed. As far as the police were concern, it was not a crime of the sexual nature. Although there was a wound in the neck and throat area. The injuries were not large but small. Something was definitely stabbed in there so many times. It could not be determined if that was what actually killed her or she was drown. But one thing was certain, from that moment, the investigators were sure that was not a natural death. So all necessary precaution were taken. The investigators always begin with the worst case scenario, so they start assuming it to be a crime.

Chapter 2

They worked according to the rules so that they do not overlooked crucial evidence. The police gather all the evidence they can find in the crime scene and mark each item with an exhibit number. To do a thorough search on such a large crime scene, it usually take some time. After all the evidence was marked, the investigators turned the body over and blot it out of the river. It is very important to them to get the body out of the water intact as possible. And then search it to identify the victim. That was how the investigators began their investigations. If you have a victim without any identification, there could be nothing for the investigators to start with. In searching the victim's cloths, Remy discovered some small balls of paper in her jeans pocket. It was a piece of white paper with a telephone number written on it. It was written in ink and still eligible. Water has not destroyed it. Another paper was unraveled and it was a bus transfer ticket.

Remy photographed the evidences at the crime scene, and they transcribed the details to the investigators immediately. They dried the paper overnight and send it to the exhibit room to be used as evidence. The body of the teenager was removed from the crime scene and pronounced dead by the police and transported to the morgue at Manchester city general hospital. The police needed to established where the stabbing was hold. When they consider the current and weight of the river, the body would not have moved a great distance. They looked for things that may directly involved like a weapon or anything. The search for clues continues for hours. At one point, Remy makes a curious discovery. An engraved on the chunk of a tree was a description "Milo, TP". He advised the chief investigator about the carving but nothing came out at that time.

Remy completes his forensic investigation on the crime scene and went to the morgue. The next day the body was transported from the morgue to London for further investigation. Remy made sure that he had not missed anything during the search of the clothing, and that the victim's hand is well protected incase the found traces of the murder DNA. He also took finger print photographs. At the scene it was impossible to take finger prints photographs, giving the recent condition of the victim's finger, being taken out of water, Remy inflate the skin. He used a syringe to inject water under the skin, and the finger would appear normal. He spayed some ink on the finger and took the finger print. At that moment the print was quite good. The print he took from the middle finger was very good. Despite her obvious young age, no one reported that she was missing before her dead body was found.

Who is she, how did she come to such a tragic end? The body of a teenager was stabbed into the neck and her body was found faced down in the Manchester river. Her identity remains unknown. There have been no report about a missing person in the region. Examining the piece of paper found in the victim's pant, detective sergeant John begins his search for the killer. Once they have finished with the crime scene, they began on the investigation to establish between the name and phone number found on the piece of paper. Because there was no other identification. They later found the address corresponding to the phone number which was a young woman name Helen, living in Manchester. Two of the investigators detective John and Mary went to speak with the Helen. They showed her the victim's photograph and cloths. She confirms the cloths belongs to her and that she loaned them to Shelly. She also said that she recently met Shelly and agreed that she stays with her. Shelly later left her apartment and never returned to her. She loaned the cloths to Shelly on May 30, 2006. In addition, Shelly said she was going to see her boyfriend. Helen sensed that Shelly was nervous on going back to her boyfriend. The investigators learned that Shelly has been placed in the youth center and she escaped. She was only 15 years old. The detective immediately contacted the youth center. An official from the youth center came to the morgue to identify the body.

Shelly was positively identified as one of their charges. Following confirmation of the victim's identification, they now have names and contacts of people who knew the victim including the victim parents. The police visited the victim's parents and broke the sad news to them about the death of their daughter Shelly. Mr. Any Morgan,

Shelly' father thought she was still at the youth center with her elder sister, not knowing that she had escaped and neither did the center nor her elder sister told him about the disappearance of Shelly. He later asked the police to do everything with their power to find who murdered Shelly. The police left him and continued with their investigation. The investigators met with all the people who were friends with the victim. They knew all what she did and who she met up with, until her death. One of the key person the detectives questioned was Shelly elder sister Regina Morgan, who was also in the youth center. She said she knew Shelly had escaped but hoping she would come back. Regina also told the detectives that Shelly was dating a person called Tony. He and Shelly reportedly lived together. Apparently, Shelly wanted to return to Liverpool, her hometown to live with her grandmother. Tony allegedly threatened to kill her if she left him.

Two detectives was sent to meet Tony, inviting him to their office for questioning. Tony said he was not interested in doing that. Nevertheless, after speaking with his lawyer, he finally agreed to surrender himself to the police for questioning. Tony said he has not seen Shelly for over a week. He kept on denying and proving to be innocent. All the information the police has gotten so far points that Tony was the prime suspect. But what the investigators need now is to prove that Tony is the killer. There are many autopsy reports available for the investigation. Jane was a forensic biologist. She works on the Shelly's case. Swaps were taken from her neck and taken to the pathologist. The result of the test indicated that there was no evidence of semen's at all. Actually when there is a crime like this, they investigate whether there is a sexual assault.

Investigation further reveals that there was no male profile associated with the victim's body. They found no blood or toxicology, and the alcohol content was negative. The found eight small wounds, about half a centimeter wide on the right side of the victim's neck. At least two of the wound have punctured the artery. It could have been fatal. However, the official caused of the death was attributed to drowning. So while the stabbed wound in the neck was created by a single edge blade, the victim actually downed. That was the cause of the death. After the stabbed, did the victim drowned by Tony, or she drowned while looking for help? When the police met with detective Mary, she said when she first met with the suspect Tony, he had a knife. This knife was very similar with the one that causes the injuries on the victim's neck. Finding the knife was a priority for detective sergeant John. Andy, Shelly's father on the other hand went to the youth center to see his daughter Regina. He met and quarrel with her for not telling him that Shelly had escaped from the youth center. He then took Regina home. At home, Andy asked Regina to tell him all she knows about the whole matter. Regina then told him that all she knows is that Shelly had a boyfriend called Toney, and any time she ran away from home; she usually went to Tony's apartment to stay with him. She gave her father the address of Tony's apartment. Andy went to visit Tony in his apartment to hear his own side of the story. On getting there, he discovered that Tony no longer lives in that apartment, for he had already vacated the apartment and now living with his mother. Andy being confused and did not know what to do, decided to take law into his own hands, by hiring a private detective to search for Tony's mother house address and Tony himself. He later discovered where Tony lives and went there to see both Tony and her mother. Unfortunately, Tony had fled to Paris, France to live with his friends. Al he does in Paris is clubbing, partying and doing drugs. He lives a lavish life and very violent. When Andy got to Tony's mother house he could not see Tony. He then threatened her to produce Tony within a week or else he would kill her. He accused Tony for killing her daughter Shelly. He believe Tony is the only prime suspect.

Tony and her mother used to communicate while in Paris. Her mother called him and told him what happened. How Andy came to her house and ordered her to produce him Tony, within a week else he would kill her. Hearing this Tony was mad and decided to take down Andy and even his wife and Regina. He then hired three assassins to take down the whole family. He gave them photographs of them all. The assassins first got to the youth center searching for Regina not knowing that she is no longer there. A person they asked of her directed them to one Regina Adams, a look alike, as they did not mention her surname, so the person did not know that it was Regina Morgan they were looking for. Regina Adams is the daughter of Remy Adams, the forensic investigator. They took note of her and waited patiently until she comes out during lunch break. The got her kidnapped into a van, took her away, killed and dumped her inside a river. A colleague of hers who saw the drama ran to her teacher and reported the mater. The teacher then called the police.

The police arrived and started asking questions. They watched the CCTV to get any clues that will help them in the investigation. On watching the CCTV, the saw the face of the assassin asking about Regina, and also the van and the plate number. With all these information the police were able to trace the owner of the van who runs a car rental business. He told the police that three men came and rented the van. He gave the police of the name of the particular one that rented the van as Richard Bush. He indeed used a fake name. After the police search their database for Richard Bush, they discovered there was no such name. Then they realized that he might have given out a fake name. They later made it known to Remy Adams that his daughter had been kidnapped and the van has been recovered. Remy being a forensic specialist came quickly and did a thorough forensic investigation on the van. Took all the finger print on the van including the steering and seats to the laboratory. After analyzing them, he made a huge discovery. He got all the names and contact information of the three assassins. He immediately gave them to the police. The police hunted for them and got all of them arrested. They were all taken to the police station for questioning. At the end, they confessed that they were hired by Tony all the way from Paris, France to take down Andy and his entire family. Unfortunately, for them, they killed the wrong Regina. They also took the police to the river where they dumped her body. They recovered the victim's body and took her to the morgue. They also used the service of the Interpol to track Tony in Paris and got him arrested. Tony was brought back to Manchester, England to face his crime.

Chapter 3

On the other hand, the investigators continue in Shelly's case, being that they have to prove it in the law court that it was Tony who killed Shelly. Because the investigations is in its each stages, the investigators must take important all evidence provided for them. To prepare a strong case, they must determine the accuracy of each clue, and establish its importance. The victim has a history of self-harm, which is problematic in creating a case. They have to remove the probability that the victim stabbed herself. To eliminate that probability they had to find the knife at the scene. They search the river and the crime scene with a metal detector and water barrier. Shelly was 15 when she ran away from a young woman's shelter. After searching no weapon was found. That proved that they victim has not committed suicide else the murder weapon would have been found on the crime scene. Since they did not find any weapon on the crime scene, it is believe that the assailant took the weapon with him.

Next is to recover the knife that was seen in possession of the suspect. The detectives ordered the search of the apartment Tony and Shelly had lived together. Ten days after the body of the victim was found, the suspect gave up his apartment in Manchester, and went back to live with his mother. Since the suspect no longer live in the apartment, a warrant was given to the investigators to carried out a thorough search and investigation on the apartment. Because the suspect was no longer living in the apartment, it became easier to carry out investigation on the apartment. The goal of the investigator is to determine if the crime was committed in the apartment.

Jane, a forensic biologist was assigned to do the investigation in the apartment. She takes samples and biological examination of substances. Determine the nature of the biological substance, and when necessary, she does a genetic study. She determine the genetic profile of biological substances, and compare that to the victim. That way one can find the victim's blood. For instance on the suspects clothing, or a weapon, or the victim's virginal, which could be compared to the genetic profile for the suspect they have obtained a warrant arrest for. She started working on Shelly's case nearly three weeks after her discovery. Investigators have made lots progress in the investigation. Jane was asked to search for bloodstains in the residence Shelly shared with her boyfriend Tony. It was a little small empty two-bedroom apartment. All she had to do is to search for blood on the floors, walls, in the bathroom, and on the matrass that was left there. She found two tiny spots of blood on the matrass.

She then found on drop of blood on the frame of the bathroom. The spots of blood on the matrass was about two centimeters in diameter. She cut off the part of the matrass having the spots of blood, and took it to the laboratory for examination and analysis. She had them extracted to obtain DNA, and amplified them to get a genetic profile. She also took a blood sample from the victim for comparison. The spots of blood on the matrass gave a combination of genetic profile which was similar to what they would obtain if she took that man combined to the DNA profile of Shelly. The same man who left his drop of blood on the door frame and the two spots on the matrass. So it was two small spots, and cannot confirm from the spots that the crime happened in the apartment.

Because they knew from the investigation, that Shelly slept there. It could have been menstruation blood. Following the analysis of the suspect apartment, the investigators cannot conclude that there was a significant spill connected to the homicide or death of Shelly. For investigators, it is evident that the crime was committed at the Manchester River. Shelly's cloths were returned from the forensic lab, dried and searched the pocket again by the investigators. In the pants pocket, they found two more pieces of small ball papers. The papers were dry, making it impossible to work with. On June 17, the police conducted a second search, this time on Tony's motherhouse where he lived after giving up his apartment.

The police needs to recover all the properties of Shelly that are in Tony's possession in hope to find the DNA. Finally, the investigators found the knife Tony had on his key chain. They sent it to the laboratory forensic lab in London. Jane began her forensic investigation. She searched for blood on the clothing, boots, shoes and they were negative. She made a report to that. Upon visual examination on the knife, there were no blood stains. It was a small retractable knife. The blade in the knife was similar to the length and size the pathologist wrote on his report about the wound on the victim's neck. She used the testing substance to detect stains of blood on the knife, even if it is invisible to the eyes.

The knife has been washed. In opening the plastic knife handle, she found bits of dry blood and it found out to match the genetic profile of the victim. That was how the investigators were able to link the knife from their suspect. To the victim. That was a major break through for the investigators. However, they still must remove any possibility of doubt. In this case, there are no witness only the suspect knows the truth. When the police interrogate him, they must be aware of every piece of evidence, direct or circumstantial. They must be able to demonstrate that the suspect is guilty. Meanwhile, Remy decided to examine the balls of paper found in Shelly's clothing, following the autopsy. He brought them to the laboratory, put them into the water so that they can be soft. The next day, they have to be in water for 20 hours, and he gently open them. He realized that these two pieces of papers, went with the first bus transfer. There were two pieces of the transfer, and completed it.

Remy can now make out everything on the bus ticket. He assemble the pieces of ticket in such a way that he can take photographs on the entire ticket, and gave it to the investigators to add to the file. The investigators met with the bus drivers who punch the tickets but he has no memory of Shelly, because many people take the bus. The bus ticket corroborated with the statement of the woman that loaned her cloths to Shelly on the day she was last seen alive. It prove that on the June 30th of last year, Shelly took the bus down town on the direction of Tony her boyfriend. The next element to be resolve is the carving on the tree. Remy remembered that on the day he found the victim, he photographed the tree. In the picture, you could find a picture that is about 5 by 10 centimeter high.

During the investigation, the investigators learned that Milio was Tony nick name. Finding that hard that with the nick name of the suspect and the victim, gave us the impression that they knew this area. Which was very important to press charges against Tony. After reviewing the photos of the carved nick name on the tree, the investigators went to the faculty of forestry, at the university of Manchester to meet with a forest pathologist to carry out an autopsy on the engraving on the tree. The pathologist concluded the test on the to determine when was the carving made. He concluded that the carving was made at the same time that the murder occurred. This represent a step to the right direction in pursuit of the killer. From the outcome of the autopsy, the suspect was already targeted from the history of his violence, drug addiction and threat he made to the victim and the knife they have seen in his possession. He was the prime suspect of Shelly's murder. The investigators decided to proceed with the interrogation of the suspect. But before they would do that, they must try to eliminate all other possibilities. Because for this murder, they have no witnesses. They have got the victim who cannot speak anymore. And there is only the accused who can tell us what really happened. So they eliminated all possibilities that there could be anyone else who killed the victim. The investigators along with the prosecutions prepare to meet the suspect in detention. The suspect and the three assassins were detained, waiting to face charges of the murder of Regina Adams. They explain their evidence to him, and he confess that he is ready to face charges. We have every reason to believe that he committed the crime. After they have all details in the file, they made Tony to make the final confession on how he killed Shelly.

The Detectives started interrogating him. The interrogation lasted for about 10 hours. After that, the suspect broke down. He decided to open up and tell the police what happened on the day of the murder. The police cautioned him that he wants to tell them about the murder of the victim, he can, but he has the right to call his lawyer first. Tony said no, he did not want to call his lawyer anymore, that he wanted to recount what happened. He said that they visited the riverbank, on the place where the police found the carved tree. That was the place where he and Shelly like to be together because he was in love with her. He accused Shelly of being a prostitute out of jealousy. They both argued. He got angry and brought out his knife, opened it while Shelly was running away because she was scared. He chased her and caught her, stabbed her multiple times on the neck.

While Shelly was crawling away, he left the scene. He never admitted putting her into the river. He never try to find out if she needed help. He did not want to explain more than that. He said it happened in the riverside where they swore their love to each other. He said he left the scene and returned two days later to try to find the chain that he lost, during the fight with the victim. He said he found the chain at the scene. If he had not find the chain at the scene, the investigators would have found it. At the law court, Tony and the three assassins were sentenced to life in prison for third degree murder. The investigators put on a brilliant performance. Water almost erased the evidence. However, due to their perseverance and determination, they were able to unravel the mystery behind the murder of Shelly Morgan and Regina Adams.

Will To Kill

Chapter 1

It was a hot night about 11:30 pm, November 2005; a murder took place in this Brazilian apartment. The victim was an American businessman. His death would transform the life of his mother. Every mother would know what it feels like to lose a child. It is just feel with pain. Esther was on trial in Brasilia, the Brazilian capital. She always protest her innocent and never agreed she had committed any crime. However, her mother in-law have spent three years fighting to get her in the dark.

Mike Farrell 25 years old grew up with two of his younger sisters Ruth 21 and Kate 18, in Los Angeles, California, United States of America. Things changed when his father died. Mike was 15 years old then. He was quite a playful brother when my dad died by a motor accident, said Ruth, one of his younger sister. Previously, life was tough at Mike. He was so taken with his computer. Mike got his first job working with computer in Los Angeles. His future bride Esther was growing up in the other world. Favela is a slum area in Rio de Janeiro, Brazil. The people living there are very poor. There is no running water, electricity, or sanitation. According to Esther's mother, Maria Carlos, Esther was a very good girl, she was well behaved when she was young. She spent most of her time in the house. When her father was ill, she did the washing and help make mat to sell.

She was a talkative when she was small. She dreamt of being a bar girl, believing one day she could marry an American, said Monica Robinho, Esther's aunt. When Mike was 25, he was offered an exciting job in Leblon, Rio de Janeiro, Brazil, as a computer technician and analyst. A computer company promised to triple his salary if he left Los Angeles, California, to live and work in Leblon, Rio de Janeiro, Brazil.

Leblon is a vibrant, cosmopolitan district in Rio de Janeiro. It's been featured in many Brazilian soap operas, making it one of the city's most famous neighborhoods. Its fame is completely justified! There are many attractions, natural beauties, and fun options for things to do and see while you're here. While most Rio de Janeiro neighborhoods have names of indigenous origin like "Copacabana" and "Ipanema", Leblon has a French-sounding name. Why is that? In 1845, the name "Leblon" was given as a tribute to a Frenchman who lived in Rio de Janeiro. His name was Charles Le Blond, an important businessman who owned a lot of land in the city and bought acreage in the Leblon region with the intent of opening a whaling company. Despite the area's beautiful natural landscapes, the neighborhood was considered an undesirable place to live because it was too far from downtown Rio and too inaccessible due to the absence of streetcar lines. Who would have thought that years later Leblon would become one of the most desired and valued neighborhoods in Rio de Janeiro, associated with sophistication and famous people sunbathing while they contemplate the beautiful Morro Dois Irmãos?

If you want a taste of the authentic Leblon experience, pay a visit to Bar Jobi. This restaurant bar has been serving traditional Portuguese-Brazilian recipes since 1956. Dishes like the delicious bolinhos de bacalhau (small codfish cakes) are what keep this establishment brimming with happy customers. The Bracarense is another Leblon favorite. Since its opening in 1961, it has been attracting Cariocas and international tourists alike. Once you've treated yourself to a delicious Brazilian snack, take the opportunity to visit Leblon Beach, only 2 blocks away. The area has never been so attractive. Those that aren't there want to get in, and those who are will not leave. It's the Beverly Hills of Latin America, but in less than 15% of the total area occupied by the California city. And that's what makes Leblon so exclusive. Leblon is a neighborhood located next to Ipanema. You probably at least heard the song "Girl from Ipanema" performed by Frank Sinatra and Tom Jobim? Well, Ipanema is indeed that trendy place where not only girls but every teenager and young adult wants to hang out. The beach is vibrant with hundreds of people every time of the day either getting a tan or exercising in their bathing suits. And the community has great bars, restaurants and condos which are hot places to see and be seen.

For decades Leblon never had the same hype. It had always been the quiet place down the beach squeezed in the 2.15 km2 (0.83 sq mi) between Ipanema, Lagoa, Gávea, Vidigal and the ocean. Traditionally it has always been the family type of neighborhood, where everybody knows each other, kids go to the same schools and their parents to the same clubs, the same stores and the same beach. Until it started being constantly featured in the most famous Brazilian soap operas (soaps are huge in the country. Everybody watches and talks about them everywhere, especially at work!). Coincidence or not, the fact is that Leblon has suddenly exploded in the late 2000s. At the same time the whole country of Brazil experienced a boom in the economy, but in Leblon the effect became much more evident. Prices in general went through the roof: a rent for a 2-3 bedroom condo jumped from 1000-1200 reais (U$ 370-440) to 5000-6000 reais (US$ 1850-2200). The price of meals, clothes, goods and entertainment in general have doubled in about 8 years (which is of course way above inflation). Every real estate owner in Leblon is now considered a millionaire, as nothing costs less than 1 million. So much so that the neighborhood is regarded as having the most expensive price per residential square meter/square footage in Latin America, rivaling Manhatan.

Rio has a shocking reputation, but ordinary street crime is the problem you are most likely to encounter. A few simple rules can significantly reduce the likelihood of an assault. Never go out wearing valuable jewellery or watches; keep cameras and mobile 'phones out of sight; don't speak loudly in English in public places; keep car doors locked and windows shut when out and about; and above all, keep an eye on what is happening around you at all times. If challenged, always hand over everything without a fight – including your car. It is always worth having some cash to hand over, if challenged, but never go out with a large amount. All that said, most expatriates live a perfectly normal life in Rio and do not have any problems. Weatherwise, Rio is a steamy, tropical city with high humidity levels year-round. Summer (Dec-March) is the hottest and stickiest time of year. Temperatures generally hover between 35-40°C, although it can get hotter and there is a lot of rain. Frequently,

Rio's great landmarks are hiding in the cloud, which can be a big frustration for visitors.

Most homes only have air-conditioning in the bedrooms, although hotels, offices, schools and public buildings tend to be air-conditioned throughout. In the winter (Jun-Sept) the sun shines, the skies are blue and temperatures usually stay around 25°C, although it can be much cooler, particularly in the mornings and evenings. Anything below 20°C is considered cold and out come the woolly tights, anoraks and electric blankets. You will have the swimming pool to yourself. Spring (Sept-Dec) is notable mainly for the rain and the cold fronts which sweep up from the Antarctic on a relatively regular – and refreshing – basis. The high humidity levels tend to be beneficial for asthma sufferers, although they lead to a constant battle against mould in the house. Doors and windows need to be opened regularly and some people use dehumidifiers on a daily basis. Most people have had the experience of taking something out of the wardrobe, which they haven't worn for a long time, and finding it has a soft green coating! It is better to leave precious books or pictures in storage at home, rather than bring them to Rio.

Chapter 2

Natives of Rio are known as cariocas - and there are a lot of them! Rio is Brazil's second city in terms of size, after São Paulo. The population officially stands at 7 million, although the real figure for the metroplitan area could be double that. A sizeable proportion of these people – many of them arrivals from elsewhere in Brazil – live in favelas, the sprawling shanty towns which have brought Rio so much notoriety in recent years. Favelas are dangerous places into which no foreigner, however well-intentioned, should venture unaccompanied by a local. Most are controlled by traficantes (drug traffickers), who enforce their own discipline in the community, often through acts of extreme violence. Rio's geography means that often, not much physically separates the rich from the poor – many favelas are squeezed in alongside the city's prosperous districts, and straggle precariously up the sides of the mountains. Favelas have also grown up alongside the new buildings in Barra da Tijuca, but as yet, the problems are not so serious – space and the sheer speed of development have reduced the opportunities for establishing slum communities.

Since the worldwide economic crash, there has been a notable growth in the number of homeless people sleeping rough in Rio. On the whole, cariocas (local residents) are friendly, charming, generous and very easy to get along with. It is, however, important to be aware that time-keeping, particularly in social situations, is not a strong point – it is quite normal for Brazilians to arrive at an event two hours or more after the time specified on the invitation. Expatriates wanting to know whether or not they should arrive politely late will often ask if the event is horário brasileiro (Brazilian time – in other words late). Brazilians tend to socialize in bars and restaurants – it is not that common to be invited to their homes. Most Brazilians will assume that English speakers are American, unless advised otherwise.

His mother Mabel encouraged him so much. She felt Mike was very strong, very intelligent, and could do a lot with his life. After Mike arrived in Rio de Janeiro to start his new job, he took a new hobby. He joined the boat club in Rio de Janeiro, Brazil. That is where many professionals come to party. The club had a pub, visited by Mike often. He found himself surrounded by pretty women. Many of the women liked him because he was very handsome, and cute. He is a rich big person with blond hair. He usually crack jocks and make them laugh. Like Mike, Esther Carlos, 16 years old, lives with her parents in the slum of Favela. She came from a very poor family. She had the intention of going to school but because her parents were so poor, decided to leave home for new opportunities in the city of Rio de Janeiro. She was only 16. Her mother cried when she started working as a stripper in the bar club, because she was very young. She said she had to work because we were very poor. It is a two days journey by bus and boat to Leblon, Rio de Janeiro from Favela.

It is where many young girls like Esther comes for work as strippers. Leblon, is known as one of the sex city in Brazil. The girls there work in the bars as strippers to earn and send money back home. They lie for their age to get a job. Most of them are as young as 13. Then earned about $3 a night for dancing, and $10 if they have sex with a customer. The bar owner keep watch on them. He takes the lion share on what clients pay. Esther's elder sister Sarah said that it was kind of embossing to her for what Esther was doing. She said Esther was forced into it. She would use drugs to help her cope with the situation. The only way out for these girls is to get a wealthy boyfriend. Esther was one of the lucky ones. The dream of being rescued by a rich man is about to come true.

favela is a slum or shantytown located within or on the outskirts of the country's large cities, especially Rio de Janeiro, inhibited by mainly poor people. People living in favelas are associated with extreme poverty, because people only live in favelas when they cannot afford proper housing in the city. Favelas often lack working water and sanitation systems, educational opportunities are limited, and jobs that pay more than poverty wages are few and far between. The poverty in the favelas, it's something that's like a curse. A favela typically comes into being when squatters occupy vacant land at the edge of a city and construct shanties of salvaged or stolen materials.

The communities of favelas do not have any organization or sanitation systems and are built illegally. With a lack of any structure or legal system which leads to higher crime rates, favelas are often sites of crime and drug-related violence.

Some have identified the origins of the favela in the Brazilian communities formed by impoverished former slaves in the late 19th century, but it was the great wave of migration from the countryside to the cities from the 1940s to the 1970s that was primarily responsible for the proliferation of favelas in Brazil. Poor and confronted with exorbitant costs for scarce land and housing, those rural migrants had little choice but to become squatters. From 1950 to 1980 the number of people living in favelas in Rio de Janeiro alone increased from about 170,000 to more than 600,000, and by the early 21st century it was estimated that there were as many as 1,000 favelas there. According to the 2010 census, 6 percent of Brazil's total population lived in favelas.

Favelas are located most often on the periphery of large cities. Some of the best-known favelas are those that cling to steep hillsides in Rio de Janeiro. Favela housing generally begins with makeshift structures fashioned from wood scraps and daub. Over time more-durable materials such as brick, cinder blocks, and sheet metal are incorporated. The lack of infrastructure gives rise to improvised and jerry-rigged plumbing and electrical wiring. Often water must be ported great distances, and rudimentary methods of waste disposal pose health hazards. As a result of the crowding, unsanitary conditions, poor nutrition, and pollution, disease is rampant in the poorer favelas, and infant mortality rates are high.

A wide variety of small businesses exist in favelas and serve the needs of the community, but the favelas are also frequently crime-ridden and have long been dominated by gangs immersed in illegal drug trafficking. Police presence is sporadic, and local militias have developed in response to the gangs—only to supplant them in some cases in exploiting the favelados, as the residents of the favelas are known. An array of social and religious organizations have also developed in favelas, as have associations targeted at obtaining rights and services. Over the years the Brazilian government has taken a number of different approaches in dealing with favelas, from programs to eradicate the favelas to efforts to provide or improve infrastructure and permanent housing.

Mike mother said that Mike told her that he met Esther in the bar and that he had already fallen in love with her. Mabel was very naïve at that time. Mike fell in love with Esther, the moment he saw her. He took her out for the night, then paid the bar owner $1,000, so she would never had to return to the bar again as a stripper and a prostitute. Esther aunt said that Mike was kind, handsome as was not an old man. He was young like her and have plenty of money. According to Mabel, she was very disappointed at Mike that he brought a prostitute home. However, she has to be there to understand the situation and as a mom, she could perceive how pretty and attractive those girls could be. For they do not deserved what they are doing if not for poverty. Mike said that he had rescued one girl from that bar's terrible life.

Esther Farrell is on trial in Brazil for murdering her American husband, Mike Farrell. She claims she is innocent. Esther was 16 and Mike was 8 years older than she was. Mike's mother Mabel travelled to Brazil and met Esther. She felt Mike was feeling very safe with that relationship with Esther. He was the provider. He believes that Esther would not have dump him because without him, Esther would not have had anything. Mabel was invited for Mike and Esther's honeymoon. They went to a tropical island Ilha Grande.

Ilha Grande has been deemed one of the most beautiful islands in Brazil. A state park covering 193 square kilometres where rugged landscapes and luscious Atlantic rainforest meet scenic beaches and crystal clear waters. Cars are not permitted on the island so transport relies on boats and trekking through forest trails. You can walk around the whole island, but it would take around four days – it's not called 'The Big Island' for nothing. Most people visit Abraão, the largest village on the island, however we were longing for something a little, well more 'deserted tropical island-esque' and the pristine Praia Vermelha (Red Beach) ticked all our boxes. Ilha Grande is one of Brazil's most beautiful islands. The island is surrounded by pristine beaches, crystal clear waters, and an array of wildlife. To put it simply, Ilha Grande is an island paradise.

Mabel was worried of what she saw. She realized that Esther was not reciprocating her love to Mike. On the other hand, Esther said, Mike told her that Mabel does not want her to get married to Mike. Mike said that he loves Esther. She is the one to be the mother of his kids. Mike's hope comes true. First Jane was born, then two years later, Tommy was born. The family moved from to a bigger apartment in Leblon, Rio de Janeiro. The apartment was close to the boat bar club, where Esther used to work as a stripper and a prostitute earning $3 a night. Now she is in a different world. They rented a house in one of the most expensive neighbourhood. Mike was earning about $200,000 a year, as a computer technician and analyst. He gave Esther, a monthly allowance of $2,000. Mabel said nothing was too good for her. She was telling Mike that his wife was very lazy, because she lie on the bed all day and the maid in the house will take care of the children. Mike employed a maid to do the house work for Esther. Esther would not physically do anything. Mike said that Esther would not have to do anything for she is his princess. She was not the same Esther as she used to be, being that she feels very rich, said Monica Robinho, Esther's aunt. Because of her money, she looked down on her relatives.

It was not only Esther's life that was transformed but also life of her parents in the slum of Favela. Mike was sending them large amount of money, enough to buy a fishing boat, and to build the only brick house in Favela. He pays their fares to visit him and Esther in their new apartment and sometimes, they stayed for several weeks. Anytime Esther's parents leave something will go missing, and Esther will say it is okay, let us go buy some more. Mabel visits Mike once a year. One her visits, she noticed that her daughter in-law was acting suspiciously. She has developed the habit of sending text messages and communicating with someone. Her attitude changed and she was very angry with Mike all the time without any genuine reason. Mabel and her new husband Daniel, was not the only one suspecting that Esther was having an affair with another man. Her sister Gina has moved in as a house help to work with Mike's children. She confronted Esther about the rumours. She finally admitted to her sister that indeed the rumour was true. In addition, that she have a lover called Mario Zico, security man. She also told her sister Gina that Mike and she were having problems. The man in question was a local security guard, earning about $2,000 a year. That was the size of Esther's monthly allowance. His name is Mario Zico.

Mike was becoming increasingly suspicious of his wife behavior. Money was going missing. He gave money to Esther to take the children to a private school. One day he decided to take the children to school himself. Mike was telling his mother that Esther has really messed up this time, and that she is pulling the wedding ring. Esther was buying things for her boyfriend, even bought him a motor bike. Mike started to spend time away from his family, with his single friends. They went out to the bars and club he used to go to before he was married. One day he told Esther that he was going for business. He went to his friend's house partying with girls, but no affair. This was the last home video Mike recorded, weeks before his murder.

Mike still want his marriage to work. He gave Esther an ultimatum, to get a job or go back to school. Nevertheless, nothing changed. Therefore, he threatened her with divorce. She was faced with going back as a stripper and a prostitute in the bar. She would be back where she was before five years ago, selling herself to strangers, or living in poverty with her parents, after having being the queen. Mike decided to stop Esther's allowance. Now Esther was not able to support the large network of friends, families that came to depend on her. Mike believes that they would not hurt him because he is the golden goose, but he forgot that the golden goose could be killed. Mabel and Daniel would always remember their last holiday with Mike. Esther knew she was going to kill Mike as she says goodbye to Mabel and Daniel, who after visiting Mike and his family were heading back to the United States.

On October 27, 2012, Mabel got the news that every mother dreads. She was with Daniel. Daniel was at that time doing the garden. She got a telephone call from John, one of Mike's friend that Mike is dead. That night, Mike and Daniel have been staying in Brasilia at their business apartment. Daniel woke up when three men broke in. One held a gun to his head and said is this him, when he was told no, he went to the room where Mike was sleeping. At that, Daniel heard a yield, and three or four shots. When the shooters had left the apartment, Daniel went to Mike's room and found him dead.

Chapter 3

He went down stairs to meet the neighbours and called the police. He said to the neighbours, that fucking beach killed him. Daniel later met Esther but she was shedding crocodile tears claiming to be innocent. On hearing the sad news, Mabel said there were no evidence to link the murder to Esther at first and that it was just pure suspicion. I could not see it, she said. I knew she was arrogant and ignorant, but a murderer, I could not see it. As soon as Mabel heard of her son's murder, she flew to Brazil. At the funeral, she noticed the widow was acting suspiciously. When they went to Mike's coffin, Esther never came to them. She did not even bother about them, rather waiting for the whole scenario to die down and then fulfil her hidden agenda, which is to inherit all Mike's money. She was never upset and never shedding tears. Suddenly, she came to Mabel, asking if she had seen Daniel. Mabel said no that she had not seen anybody. Esther was trying to make it looked like Daniel murdered Mike, being his coworker.

The police investigation was moving very slowly. There is suspicions that someone connected to Mike in his place of work might have killed him. The employees said that Mike was a very good employer and do not think anybody would have done that to him. Mabel took things into her own hand. She was not going back to the United States until she had gotten justice. She hired a private detective. A former police officer who does not want to be identified. The detective carried out two hours surveillance on Esther. He discovered that there were two men who paid regular visits to her home. One of them is Esther's lover. The other his friend, another security guard. Mabel pass this information to the police, who called both men in for questioning. Daniel was able to identify them as the two of the three men who broke into his apartment the day Mike was murdered.

The two men were arrested. However, Mabel campaign to hunt Mike's killer was putting her life and Daniel at risk. She was warned that they were in danger. Friends of the accused knew who they were.

After two months, it was time to go back home. Mabel and was not going to leave Brazil without something of Mike, his children. She wanted to take Jane and Tommy home, to live with her. Because their mother was dangerous, she did not care. Mabel persuaded Esther to let Jane stay with her for the weekend. Three days later she left Brazil for the United States with Jane, her four year old daughter. She had not been able to find her grandson. She did not wanted to leave Tommy. It was the hardest thing to do, to leave him behind.

Therefore, she left passport for Tommy. Next on Mabel list was her grandson Tommy. Tommy was staying with Esther's parents in Favela. Mabel sent her private detective to Favela, with an offer of $5,000, to hand Tommy over. Esther father cried over the child because he was going away. Nevertheless, he did not have any choice because he was poor and did not have any money to send Tommy to school. He decided to hand him over to his grandmother who is very rich and have plenty of money to take care of him and send him to school. Two months after Mabel left Brazil, she was reunited with her grandmother at the Los Angeles International airport. Esther was very worried, as she had not seen her children for over two years. They were both living with Mabel and Daniel.

For three years, Mabel worked through the night to get evidence against Esther. It was a costly business. She even had to pay the police money to interview witnesses. Altogether, she spent $70,000. She wanted justice for the murder of her son, Mike. It was Esther relative that gave Mabel the breakthrough she needed. Mabel and Daniel had made friends with them. They sent text messages. Esther's aunt Monica Robinho, had promised Mabel that she would anything to help her. She said to Mabel that she did understand that they were both mothers. Esther brother in-law, and Sarah's husband is been acting suspiciously since the death of Mike. Sarah is the elder sister to Esther, and her husband Paolo was among the three men that stormed Mike's apartment the day of the murder. He was the third man and ever since the death of Mike, he has been acting strangely. When the police tried to question him, he went into hiding. Esther's aunt knew where he was. Mabel persuaded her to turn him in to the police. Finally, he was handed over to the police. He admitted that he was the third man in the night of the murder. At last, the truth was out. He started to confess. It was around 11:30 pm, when Esther came and ask me to go with them. I did not know where we were going. I got into the car, and we headed down town. He told the police that Esther's lover Mario Zico, a friend, Esther and he drove to the apartment where Mike was staying. The three men including him got out of the car and went upstairs to Mike's flat. Esther lover was the one who pulled the trigger on Mike. He fired two shots and two more. Esther sat inside the car to act as look out.

Mabel said that Esther told everybody that Mike was a millionaire, that she would get all Mike's money when Mike was dead. The confessions made, led to the conviction of Mario Zico and his accomplice convicted for murder. They are both serving life sentences. Sarah's husband, Colin, the third man of the murder who made the confession was set free in return for providing evidence. In February 2015, Esther was arrested and charged for the murder of Mike Farrell. Even though she did not fire the gun herself, she plotted the crime and can still be found guilty of murder. The judge will decide if she planned Mike's death with her lover.

Esther denied everything. But there is strong evidence against her. The men who murdered Mike had the keys to get into Mike's apartment at the night of the murder. At the night of the murder, Esther claims she was as sleep at home. Yet a neighbor saw her come early hours of the morning. There are 14 people giving evidence against Esther. There is not a single witness to support her version of the events. She was remanded in prison for seven months. The only visitor she had was her father. The rest of her family turned against her because she had brought them to an open shame. They have given evidence that they heard her and her lover planning to murder Mike for his money. In six weeks' time, the judge will announce his verdict. The penalty for murder in Brazil is life sentence, or even death by hanging.

Monica was saying that it is such a shame for what have happened to Esther. She has wrecked her life and allowed herself to be carried away by greed. Mike's friends felt for him after his death. The judge is about to pronounce the verdict on Esther, and Mabel is determine to be there. She have waited for about three years for this moment. With no family and friends to support her, Esther has nobody to talk to but her lawyer. The judge showed up in the court and the verdict was red. Esther was fined guilty of murder, and sentenced to prison for life. She was spared the death penalty with no possibility of an early release. After the verdict, the press interviewed Mabel and she said, I do not get any pleasure seeing my daughter in-law going to prison. In addition, no matter what happens, it will never bring my son back. There is no pleasure seeing Esther going to prison. Before Mabel leaves Brazil for the United States, she went to confront Esther with her crime and to say goodbye. Esther was still with the police waiting to be transported to prison.

Mabel said to Esther, how could you convince me that you did not murdered Mike? Then Esther replied her saying, whatever must have happened to Mike I do not know. I am completely innocent. She kept on denying the whole allegations brought before her about the death and murder of Mike Farrell, the American businessman. Then said Mabel, but it was your boyfriend that pulled the trigger orchestrated by you. Esther then said, I never even have a relationship with him. Esther continues to deny everything. Mabel had hoped that she will confess, but she was so hardened in heart without any conscience. Mabel gave her some pictures of her children Jane and Tommy and then said to her, dear Esther, you are convicted in court for the murder of your husband Mike, with the help of your lover. Nothing you say will convince me you are innocent. I can now leave Brazil since justice has been done, and you will spend the next 40 years in jail.

You will be an old woman with a wasted life. You had everything. Mike calls you his princess and loved you very much. You are an evil woman with no thought of the life you have ruined. Mabel then left heft her and say goodbye.

The End

Stab In The Heart

Chapter 1

Normally, Ajit Gupta had a good job. He had a good wife, a good home, but underneath the surface, Ajit had a very dark secret. There was a very shocking incident that occurred in Ajit childhood. Ajit had a dark obsession, and that was his niece. Ajit Gupta was born on June 17, 1970. He was born in the city of Kochi, India. Kochi is one of the cosmopolitan cities of Kerala which had come into limelight with its rich treasures of spices. It is also called as the Gateway to Kerala and its awe inspiring scenic views makes it a perfect tourist destination. Kochi is small place in Kerala which is also known as God's Own Country and famous for its green pastures with beautiful landscapes. This city houses the very famous port which is known for its world class standards and facilities. International airport at Nedumbassery is located approximately 40 km North of the city. Malayalam is the native language spoken here. With economic and social development this place has become one of the most happening places in Kerala. People are highly fashion conscious and great western culture influence can be seen in the way they dress.

Kochi is a well developed city and there are different communities and caste residing in this area. As per the census of 2011 it has a population of 601,574 and a population density of 6340 people per km. Here the community comprises mostly of Malayalees, Tamilians, Gujaratis, Jews, Anglo-Indians, Sikhs, Konkanis and Tulus. The major religions practiced include Hinduism and Christianity. Other religions like Islam, Jainism, Buddhism and Sikhism are also followed by a small section of society. Being very close to the equator, Kochi has a tropical monsoon. The temperatures range between 23-31°C. Summer season is in months of March to June where the highest temperature recorded at 35°C (95°F). During June and September this place experiences heavy showers and during October – December lighter rains can also be expected. Kochi gets an average rainfall of 3,228.3 mm which is greatly contributed by the south west monsoons.

Kochi has well connected roads leading to different cities and states. The NH-47 with four lanes and in some part 6 lanes connect this city to Coimabatore, Pallakad and Trissur. The NH-17 connects to Panvel while NH-85 links Kochi to Dhanushkodi in Tamil Nadu. Transportation includes both private and public buses and auto rickshaws. The Kochi Railway system is organized and operated by the Southern Railway Zone of Indian Railways. The Ernakulam Junction and Ernakulam Town are the two prime railway stations located here. You also have smaller stations like Edapally, Aluva and some on the surburbs like at Kalamassery, Nettoor, Kumbalam and Aroor.

The backwaters are seen to operate many ferry services for both the tourists as well as the residents. Run by the Kerala water Transport Department and other private firms the houseboats caters to offer tourists different price packages that are categorized as Gold, Silver and Platinum. Earlier, they were used to transport harvest but now they have been converted into modes of transportation for people. There are small islands located between Fort Kochi and Madacherry, which can only be accessed with boats. The Kochi port provides services of managing cargo and storage facilities. Again, there are many passenger ships that are seen to operate between Colombo and Lakshadweep.

The Cochin International Airport located at Nedumbassery offers connectivity to passengers for both domestic and international flights. This airport is huge with a terminal area of 840,000 sq ft (78,000 m2) and it has the capacity to hold 1800 passengers. You can access flights to Middle East or Singapore or Malaysia or any part of the world.

Kochi is the commercial hub of Kerala and you have many industries contributing to the success of this place. You have the Kochi Refineries located at Ambalamugal which works along with the Bharat Petroleum Corporation Limited (BPCL). This refinery is a major contributor of petrol, diesel, aviation turbine fuel, LPG and many more useful bi-products. Eloor is an industrial area of Kochi where you have around 250 industries which are involved in producing retro-chemical products, fertilizer, pesticides and even leather products. The 100-acre Kochi info park is located at Kakkanad village in Ernakulam district. This IT park is under the possession of infoparks Kerala, an organization managed by the government. This project has become quite successful and within short span of time it has brought investors like Tata Consultancy Services, Wipro, Affiliated Computer Services, OPI Global, IBS Software Services and US Technology. Being a coastal region fishing is also major industry here. Seafood is packed and supplied in and around Kochi and even exported to foreign countries.

He moved to Mumbai when he was 13 years old. He live with his parents Ajish Gupta his father and Diya Gupta his mother. He has three sisters, Ishani being the eldest, then Riya and Myra being the youngest. Ajit childhood can definitely be described as destructive. His dad worked as a lobourer for a manufacturing company so he had to move around a lot. And his family move around with him so many times. They moved from Kochi, Mumbai, New Delhi, channel, Jaipur, Kolkata, Bengaluru and Kolaram. Even in the city of Mumbai they last live, they were still moving around. So Ajit had to relocate so many times and had to go to so many new schools. This had a huge impact on Ajit because he never felt settled. Whenever he went to a new school, and try to settle in, get familiar with the area, make some friends, his family will have to move again.

Mumbai (also known as Bombay, the official name until 1995) is the capital city of the Indian state of Maharashtra. Mumbai lies on the Konkan coast on the west coast of India and has a deep natural harbour. In 2008, Mumbai was named an alpha world city. It is also the wealthiest city in India, and has the highest number of millionaires and billionaires among all cities in India. The seven islands that came to constitute Mumbai were home to communities of fishing colonies of the Koli people. For centuries, the islands were under the control of successive indigenous empires before being ceded to the Portuguese Empire and subsequently to the East India Company when in 1661 Charles II of England married Catherine of Braganza and as part of her dowry Charles received the ports of Tangier and Seven Islands of Bombay. During the mid-18th century, Bombay was reshaped by the Hornby Vellard project, which undertook reclamation of the area between the seven islands from the sea. Along with construction of major roads and railways, the reclamation project, completed in 1845, transformed Bombay into a major seaport on the Arabian Sea. Bombay in the 19th century was characterised by economic and educational development. During the early 20th century it became a strong base for the Indian independence movement.

As the city that never sleeps and famous for its high-end malls and lucrative streets. Mumbai City also known as Bombay, offers unique experiences, from the beautiful promenades to the cosmopolitan culture. Mumbai India is known as the city of dreams (Mayanagri), it is the capital city of the Indian state of Maharashtra. Mumbai is also the second most populous city in India with a population of 19.98million. Moreover, it lies on the Konkan coast, which is on the west coast of India, with its very own natural harbour. Back in 2008 Mumbai was named an alpha world's city and it's the wealthiest city with the largest number of millionaires and billionaires in all of the cities in India. Generally, the city serves as headquarters to some of the financial institutions like the National Stock Exchange, Reserve Bank of India and the Mint among many others. The name Mumbai comes from Mumba or maha-Amba, which is the name of a patron goddess Mumbadevi (of the native Koli community). In the Marathi language, the name means" Mother ". However, some sources disagree with this claim, saying the name Mumbai did not originate from the goddess Mumbai.

Residents from this location are mainly referred to as Mumbaikar in Marathi. From which the suffix "kar" means "the residents to ".Over the years it grown in popularity, especially after the official name of the city was changed to Mumbai. However, older terms like Bombayite also apply. Mumbai has the most population of India and is one of the largest populated urban areas in the world. People of Mumbai are hard-working, witty and modern people. They are passionate about their lives. As Mumbai people are proud of their heritage, they prefer to dress in traditional attire, although western attire is very popular in the city of Mumbai. Mumbai city serves as a great opportunity to fantastic careers prospects. One of the reasons why most migrants from different parts of the country move to this city in search of a better life. Hence, the name City of Dreams.

Despite the different levels of wealth distributions, once inside the city, hard work always has a way of paying back for most hardworking individuals. The city of Mumbai is one of the world's largest film industries. In India, the city is an established film capital. Here is where most Bollywood stories are created. It is also where you will find their most famous directors, actors, producers and crew members in real life. Bollywood releases exciting firms which are distributed all over the globe, sharing the Hindu culture, stories and not forgetting dances. As India's largest city by population and the centre of all financial and commercial practices in the country. The municipality generates 6.16% of the total GDP, serving as an economic hub in India. Since the liberalization of 1991, India has witnessed tremendous economic growth. In 2009 and it was ranked as the most expensive office market in the world, it was also ranked among the fasted cities in that country to start a business. In terms of architecture, Mumbai exhibits one of the complexes, luxurious and outstanding architecture. Some include the Pristine White Haji Ali Dargah and the Bandra Worli Sea. The Victorian Architecture of the Chhatrapati Shivaji Terminus has been able to withstand over a century of events and is still a lucrative site.

The south of Mumbai is equipped with colonial-era buildings and soviet-style offices which offer a breathtaking view to every visitor. These brilliant masterpieces are Mumbai's unique offering to the rest of the subcontinent.

Mumbai city is blessed with numerous tourist attractions from the caves like Elephanta Cave, Kanheri Caves and the Mahakali Caves, to the beautiful studios like Bombay Talkies. Indeed, there are different sites to explore, depending on your interests and time. When it comes to hotels, you can enjoy staying in one of the most beautiful hotels depending on your financial capabilities. Some of the most beautiful hotels in Mumbai include The Oberoi Mumbai, The Taj Mahal Tower Mumbai, The Taj Lands' End, The Taj Mahal Palace, Mumbai and many more. The hotels offer some of the best services to help you relax while enjoying your stay in Mumbai. Mumbai is a beautiful, unique and spectacular location to lay low and have a good time. There are many activities to interact with making your stay extremely memorable. Ensure that you take a walk on the city's promenade, you might come across your favorite Bollywood star. Mumbai makes space for everyone and opens up opportunities to anyone willing to chase them. However, everything in this city is fast and requires time to adapt, especially if you are relocation to this location.

Mumbai, known as "the city that never sleeps," is a diverse city and one of the busiest cities in India. Festivals form an important part of Mumbai. Banganga Festival: It is basically a musical show. The festival's purpose is to promote Maharashtra's culture. Different artists come from different parts of the country. Elephants Festival: It is organized in Elephanta caves. Musicians and dancers from all over India participate in the festival. Gudhi Padwa Festival: It marks the beginning of the Hindi year. This festival is celebrated throughout the state of Maharashtra,as it is considered like the New Year celebration. People hang bamboo stuff (gudhi) on the entrance of their houses, as it is believed that gudhi provide protection from evil forces. Ganesh Chaturthi Festival: The most important festival of Maharashtra. It is a celebration of the birth anniversary of Lord Ganesha, the Elephant-God. The people celebrate this festival by bringing an idol of the lord to their homes, decorated and worship it. The festival comes to an end by carrying the idol in a huge procession to the sea and immersing it in the water, amidst drum beats, songs and dancing. Diwali Festival: It is one of the major festivals of Hindus. It presents the victory of good over bad. It is believed that Diwali festival is celebrated on the day that Lord Rama killed the demon king Ravana, completed his fourteen days of exile and returned to his kingdom. On this day, people worship Lord Ganesha and Goddess Lakshmi and seek their blessings. People clean their houses and decorate them with lights and flowers. People also burn crackers and fireworks and pray for a flourishing new year.

Chapter 2

Ajit has been described as a very shy and introvert child, and he struggle to make friends anyway. Because he finds it difficult to settle down in one school, that made it difficult for him to come out of his shell. He was an easy target for bullies in school. Upon that Ajit was also suffering at school, and he did not have it easy at home either. It is because his relationship with his father was a bit strange. Ajit's father felt that Ajit was not manly enough. In order to make his son more manly, he will take him to hunting trips, teach him how to do manly things. He would also scold Ajit, whenever he shows any emotion. Ajit was never allowed to show any emotions because that was weakness. He was never allowed to cry. But Ajit do have one comfort in his life and that was the family dog. This dog was Ajit best friend. Ajit love spending time with his dog. They were inseparable when he is at home. However, Ajit's dad had a problem with this. Ajish did not like Ajit relationship with the dog. He felt Ajit is becoming emotionally dependent on the dog. That is not manly.

What really annoyed Ajish is that the dog will always misbehaved for him, but to Ajit, the dog is perfect and well behaved. And this annoyed Ajish because he wants authority over the dog. He never once thought that he was the problem. He always get angry and shout at the dog. He was not very nice to the dog. But for Ajit, this dog was everything to him. The dog was the best friend he had in his life. But unfortunately, that would not last forever. When Ajit was 15, an incident occurred that would change his life forever. And ultimately I do believe that this is the moment that triggered of the series of event that happened in this case. I do feel that this is the trigger point. And this escalated very quickly from this moment on.

What started all of this was that one day, the whole family was on vacation and it was over the holiday period. One day Ajit and Ajish were out hunting doing manly things and they took the dog with them on their hunting trip. As they were out hunting and shooting their rifles, all of a sudden the dog ran away. The dog ran into the bushes probably because he was scared of the shooting being the first time he had followed them for hunting and hearing the noises of guns. Because the dog will not come out of the bushes, Ajish was getting really angry and impatient with him. So he pulled out his rifle, pointed it to the bushes where the dog was hiding, and just started shooting. According to Ajish, the reason why he was shooting at the bushes was to scare the dog to come out. He never intended to shoot at the dog. But unfortunately the dog was hit by one of the bullet from Ajish's rifle and it died at the spot. Ajit had just witnessed that his dad shot his dog. Ajit was very sad, that he wanted to cry but he was not allowed to cry so he had to keep that emotion in. He did not want to look like a kid before his parents. The family left the vacation some couple of days later and the dog was not with them. Ajit believed that his dad shot his dog on purpose. Ajit also felt that his dad wanted to teach him a lesson because he was too emotionally attached to the dog. He believed that it is disgusting and awful.

For why and how would his father shots bullets into a bush to try to get a dog out? The dog is clearly hiding in the bushes because he is already scared. That is not the way to get a dog out of the bush. The whole family is back at home and they have returned from vacation. Now it is the first week of school. Ajit has resumed school with a pretty dark and disturbing thought. Nobody knows what Ajit is going to do next. On September 18, 1985, one week after Ajit lust his dog, Ajit sat at home at the kitchen table just to do his homework. The rest of the family were at home as well. His father was busy shaving his beard. His mother was eight month pregnant. Ajit elder sister Ishani, was in her bedroom reading while his two younger sisters Riya and Myra, were in their bedroom sleeping. Actually, Ajit was not doing his homework as he pretended to be doing; rather he was actually forming a very disturbing plan. All of a sudden, he got up from the table, walked straight to his parents' bedroom; retrieve a gun from his father's nightstand. Ajit then heads to the bathroom where both of his parents currently are. He looked at his dad and before anyone could do anything, he started shooting at his dad. He fired three shots at his dad. His dad fell down and collapsed.

His mother started screaming and shouting no Ait no. She was screaming to Ishani to call the police. Ajit was not only going after his dad but the whole family. He turned to his mother and fired two shots into her stomach. One of the bullet tragically hit the eight-month's old unborn baby. Ajit mother also collapse in the bathtub. Ishani on the other hand, was in her bedroom reading when she heard her mother screaming calling her name to call the police. She heard the gunshots but did not have a clue of what is going on. She did not think that it was her brother who was firing those shots. She was terrified. She jumped out of her bed and run to the doorway. But Ajit was still there. He had left his parents bathroom and walked into Ishani's bedroom. He was still holding the gun. He raised the gun and point it at Ishani's head, the pulled the trigger. Ishani thought she had died as Ajit pulled the trigger, but the gun did not fire. Ajit had ran out of bullet. The scenario still was not over. As soon as Ajit realized that he had ran out of bullets, he dropped the gun and descended on Ishani, trying to strangle her to death. She was kicking and screaming, pleading with him and pleading for her life.

She was telling him, Ajit I love you, I love you, and I am your sister. She looked into his eyes and what she saw was not her brother. It was like he was possessed. It was like he was in a tranced. His eyes was very strange. She said to him again, I love you Ajit, I love you. That almost seem to wake him up and his eyes was refocus. He immediately said, what am I doing? Then Ishani said to him, what do you mean, what are you doing, you have shot your parents. Ishani was terrified about Ajit, for he has murdered his parents and now he wants to murder her. She wants to get away from him as far as she can physically do. She knows she has to play this right knowing Ajit is very capable of murdering her.

She started taking advantage of Ajit's confused state. She started to say it is okay, and everything is going to be okay. Everything is fine, we will run away together, we will always be together and I will never leave you. She told Ajit to pack up something because they were leaving; they want to run away together. Ajit agreed, so he went to pack up something's and as soon as he was out of the way, Ishani ran out of the house to a neighbour's house. Finally, she managed to escape. In the neighbour's house, she was saying, my brother has shot my parents, my brother has shot my parents, and he has killed them. Please call an ambulance. However, back in the house, what Ishani did not realize was that even though her father was shot three times, he managed to get himself up, got a phone and called the ambulance. The ambulance and the police were on their way. The ambulance arrived not too long after Ishani managed to escape from the house. They found Ajish lying on the floor and even though he was shot three times, they managed to treat him and luckily, he survived. The same cannot be said to Diya, Ajit's mother he had shot. Unfortunately, she did not survive. After receiving two gunshots on her stomach, and the eight-month-old unborn child, she finally died. She was only 38 years old.

She and the unborn child both lost their lives. If Ajit had successfully murdered Ishani, he would have no doubt murdered his two younger sisters. His father caused his anger because he murdered his dog. Ajit was still in the house packing up his things thinking he is running away with Ishani. He later realized that Ishani has fled the house. He also realized that Ishani has fled to a neighbour's house and called for help. He felt completely devastated and betrayed by Ishani. This is something definitely to note because this is another trigger for Ajit. Fortunately, at that moment, Ajit seems to give up and when the police arrived, he gave himself in. Ajit did not understood what he has done. He was later arrested by the police and interviewed. The police could not figure out why he murdered his parents. They believe Ajit had no genuine reason what so ever to have murdered his parents.

Ajit did not tell the police at that time that he killed his parents because his father killed his dog. Instead, he was giving weird statement such as; he was programmed to kill his parents. He said he loved his parents and did not want to kill them but he was programmed to kill them. Ajit was examined by two psychiatrists, because he was only 15 years old and have just murdered his mother. But the two experts examining him just concluded that Ajit had no mental illness, and no mental health problem at all. They said that he has acted on an irresistible impulse and that he had a moral defect and not a mental one. In addition, no motive have ever been found on why Ajit pulled the trigger on his parents.

Ajit has taken a gun, killed his mother and his unborn sibling. He tried to kill his father and sister, and the police said that he does not have any mental health problem. The authorities did not know what to do with Ajit at that time because he was only 15. Moreover, they could not charge him with murder. According to the law, 15 years old is too young to be charged with murder. However, the grand jury decided that he should receive psychiatry treatment because they believed that there is something wrong with him. The jury also stated that there is a significant risk to Ajit and that he could post a danger to the public at some point later down the line. Therefore, Ajit was taken to the psychiatrist hospital where he started receiving treatment. After receiving treatment in the hospital for one year, Ajit was released and free to go. After his released and true to go. After his release, he went back to live with his father and three siblings. This Ajit murdered his mother and tried to murder his father and entire family.

Ajish took the risk of bringing back Ajit into his house, hoping that he has changed. However, Ishani was terrified of Ajit. She was scared and did not want to live with him. Apparently, Ajish has completely forgiven Ajit. Ajish was the one that petitioned that Ajit should be released from the hospital. Ajish has stayed loyal to his son throughout the whole process. Ajish never spoke to Ajit nor his children and any other person about the shooting. Even after Ajit was released from the hospital, Ajish never find time to discus with Ajit about the shooting or interview him on why he wanted to kill him and the entire family to prevent history from repeating himself. Ajish never talked to Ishani about what happened and Ishani was absolutely traumatized by the event that night. Ajish never try to say to Ishani, that it will be ok; I will never let it happen again. I will keep an eye on him. Meanwhile, Ajit younger siblings where in their bedroom sleeping on the day of the incident. Ajish never told them anything not even, how their mother died. Riya and Myra was made to believe that their mother died in a car accident

Chapter 3

They had lived their whole lives up to their thirty's, thinking that their mother died in a car crash. They had no idea that actually their older brother had murdered their mother. Ishani was also never allowed to speak on what happened. Ajish wanted to keep this secret to the entire world. Therefore, no one ever talked about this. By this, it is as Ajit has gotten away with murder. After the incident, Ajit went back to school. He made some friends and was very good achiever at school and life. He was no longer thriving the way he was before he killed his mother. Everything seems to be going well with him after killing his mother. He actually graduated from high school, and later went to the university and graduated with a degree in aeronautics engineering. He went to find himself a job as a technician with air India. At the age of 29, Ajit would meet a woman that he would soon going to marry. This is a woman called Roshni Patel. Ajit was introduced to her through his best friend Rishi Doshi.

When Ajit was introduce to Roshni, they both hit it off. Both Ajit and Roshni had a wonderful relationship. It was not for long they got married. They seem to have a nice relationship that many people were envying them. They moved to a nice beach apartment in Mumbai. Everything on the outside seems great. However, as we know it is not always the case. As we already know, that Ajit have a very dark secret. He has a very dark disturbing side as well. There are definitely a few warning signs about Ajit. There are few red flag that Ajit best friend Rishi knew about Ajit, but did not exactly do much about them. It turns out that Rishi was actually the ex-husband of Ishani, the very sister that Ajit had tried to murder. Because Rishi was the ex-husband to Ishani, he knew the past of Ajit, that he was a murderer. Nevertheless, he did not seem to mind. He was still best friend to him after he had separated from Ishani. Rishi was telling Ajit that his sister Ishani broke his heart. Then Ajit said to him, I suggest getting a revenge, you should kill her, cut out her heart and eat it.

However, Rishi did not do anything. He thought that Ajit was joking. Ajit has gotten married to Roshni without telling her his past that he was a murderer. Roshni never had a clue about Ajit's past, what he had done, and capable of doing. She has no idea that her husband has actually murdered his mother. Rishi had come out, and he did try telling Ajit to tell Roshni about his past. Rishi too did not tell Roshni about Ajit's past, that he is a murderer. He murdered his mother. He probably felt that was not his responsibility. After Ajit and Roshni marriage, they went on living a normal and happy married life. One day, Ajit, Roshni and Rishi where out drinking for the night in a pub. Then Ajit went to the bathroom leaving Roshni and Rishi in the bar. Roshni then turns to Rishi and said to him, I think my husband has murdered someone. Then Rishi replied, oh how, what do you mean. Then Roshni went on to explain, that a woman was murdered not too far from their house. This woman has been decapitated and her heart has been cut out. At that very evening of the murder, Ajit was nowhere to be found. He was not at home, and he did not come home that evening. When he eventually come home, he was covered in blood. When Roshni confronted Ajit about him being covered in blood, he said he went out fishing and he cut the fishes. Then Roshni said, that does not looked like a fish blood. Nevertheless, Ajit had claimed that he had caught some fishes and he had cut them up. However, he returned home with no fishes. Therefore, Roshni was very suspicious. When Roshni was explaining all of this to Rishi, he had so many things on his mind. He knew already that Ajit was a murderer. He also knew that Ajit had joked about cutting a woman's heart and eating it. Rishi might have said right there to Roshni that she might be right.

Instead, he said to Roshni, oh, do not be worried, it is all misunderstanding. Ajit would not have done such a thing. Rishi would not want to clarify with Roshni that he knows Ajit's deep secret, about him murdering his mother. Rishi just swept it under the rug, like everybody else. Roshni was already convinced that Ajit could be responsible for that murder. She wanted to go to the police, but Rishi was the one convincing her not to. She decided to put all these incidents behind her, and never found out whether Ajit was responsible for hat murder or not. Ajit and Roshni remained happily married for 15 years, and Roshni is still in the dark about Ajit. Nevertheless, the secret and weird obsession did not end there. They both had two children, a son and a daughter. Arjum 11years old, and Durga 8 years old.

His niece again obsesses Ajit. Ajit's niece, Saanvi Rao, is a 37 years old woman. She works as an accountant with a bank. She was extremely hard working person and was described as a very social and energetic. She was very close with friends and families. She was also very close to her aunt Roshni. She will spend a lot of time with Roshni and Ajit. Nevertheless, nobody ever knew that she obsessed Ajit. Anytime Saanvi is around Ajit's home, he uses to keep calm and remain quiet, watching her. He has a creepy secret nickname for Saanvi, which is victorious secret, because she wears an underwear with the brand name victorious secret. It was strange how Ajit knew the brand of underwear Saanvi was wearing. Ajit did not only use this nickname in private but also around friends, families and many people. No one seems to find this weird.

Another obsession about Ajit was human anatomy. In Ajit's bedroom there where posters, journals, textbooks, all about human anatomy. They were really detailed and graphic stuffs. There were also in his bedroom, newspaper cuttings about human heart. On the back of the bedroom door, there was this huge poster about the human anatomy. There was no logical information on why Ajit was so upset with human anatomy. Ajit would often view necrophilia contents online. He would often Google erotic dead people online. In addition, Googling dead porn autopsy photos online. Really, upset with death. He also has huge collections of victorious secret catalogue. Despite Roshni living with Ajit in the same bedroom, she still did not know much about Ajit's secret life and obsession with his niece Saanvi. Later there was a terrible storm that struck the city and it affected the area where Ajit and Roshni where living.

People living in that area had to be evacuated. When Saanvi heard about this, she was worried about them. She phoned her aunt Roshni, asking her and her family to come and live with her for a while until the storm passes. Saanvi unfortunately did not realize the kind of man Ajit was. Ajit, Roshni and their 2 children leaves for Saanvi's house. On their way to Saanvi's house, Ajit dropped his kids with their grandmother, Radha. Radha is the mother of Roshni. In the beginning, it was so great and everything was going on well in Saanvi's house. They all had a very good time, cooking and drinking together and spending a very good time together. It was 20 November 2098; this is almost two weeks after the storm. Now the storm have passed and it is okay to go home. Roshni really wants to go home. There is no reason for them not to go home. Ajit was having none of this. He wanted to stay for one more night. Ajit indeed have a reason why he wanted to stay one more night but he did not tell neither Roshni nor Saanvi why he wanted to stay one more night. Ajit was formulating a very dark and disturbing plan. On the evening of 20 November 2098, everyone was settling down for the evening. Roshni was in the living room lying on the sofa, and Saanvi was in her bedroom. At this point Ajit went into the kitchen, retrieved some kitchen knives, and launched his brutal attack.

Ajit then turned on his wife Roshni. She was still lying on the sofa when Ajit approached her. Before Roshni could know what was going on, Ajit launched his attack on her. He stabbed her in quick succession seven times, and Roshni lost her life instantly. Nevertheless, Ajit was not finished there. After he had murdered his wife, he now turned to his niece Saanvi. The woman he had a dark obsession for the longest time. In addition, at this point, he then made his way to the master bedroom. He attacked Saanvi by stabbing her once in the chest, and she lost her life. However, unfortunately the murder was not alone for Ajit. We all knew his dark obsession with human anatomy. Following the murder, the then removed Saanvi's bloody cloths and proceeds to dismember and dissect Saanvi's body.

With the use of two separate kitchen knives, Ajit went on to decapitate Saanvi's head. He severed of her legs, removed her breast, disembowel her organs, and finally, he cuts out her heart. Tragically, it seems the attack on Saanvi was due to the humiliation of all of Ajit's sick desires and his obsession. Then after Ajit finished brutally murdering his wife and niece, he took a shower and cleaned himself off. He then made his way to the garage and hung himself. This attack on Roshni and Saanvi, seems to have come from nowhere. Comparing how Ajit murdered Saanvi to how he murdered Roshni, one could deduce the fact that his main target was Saanvi. The next day friends and families were becoming concern about Saanvi because she was the kind of person that was always in contact with them. When her friends and families did not hear from her, they were concern. Therefore, some concern friends went to her house. They were able to get into the garage. This is when they saw Ajit's body hanging from the rafters. The scene was horrific to them. They did not go into the house; rather they went straight to the police. The police arrived at the scene and went inside the house. They come across an absolute horror scene. The police found Roshni's body stabbed to death on the sofa. Then they came across Saanvi's body. Saanvi's body was stabbed to death as well. They also found Saanvi's head next to her body. They obviously also found Ajit's body. They were saying to themselves what must have happened here. They obviously figured out straight a way that it was Ajit that carried out the murder. They were just thinking to themselves, why? But why did he murdered these two women. On an initial investigation, what they found out about Ajit was that he was having a wonderful relationship with Roshni and he was just a happy normal person.

The police went down to Ajit and Roshni home and inside the house; they started to discover Ajit's dark secret and obsessions. They came across the anatomy postal at the back of the door. They came across the surgical books, the newspaper cut out about the heart, the huge collection of victorious secret catalogues. They also manage to figure out that his niece obsesses Ajit. As soon as they found out that his niece obsesses him, they thought that was the motive. The revelation did not just stop there. During the investigation, Ajit's sister Ishani, told the police all the dark secrets of her brother. She told the police that Ajit had murdered her mother, and tried to murder her father and her. From this moment after thirty years when Ajit's mother had died, that was when his two younger sisters Riya and myra, knew that their mother had not died on a car crash. She was actually murdered by their brother. This revelation was also shattering Roshni and Saanvi's families. They were furious that they did not know who Ajit was. That they did not know about his past. They were also furious that someone could just murdered someone. Though Ajit was 15 by then, but that he could able to murder his mother, taken to the hospital for a year and no one actually knows what he has done.

But things were not over just yet. Now the police has just learned about Ajit's past, and also his weird anatomy about heart removal combined with how Saanvi was murdered, and that her head was decapitated, and her heart was cut out. The police start to think for themselves that there is no way that this man has gone from killing his murder at the age of 15, till now 30 years later, this being his next murder. They were thinking with all guaranty that this man must be a serial killer. The next line of investigation for the police is thinking that there could be more victims. The police starts pouring over his cold cases. They also learned that in Ajit's job, he travels a lot. Which gave him many opportunities to have a lot of victims. When the police were looking into Ajit's criminal records, they discovered that 26 murders are linked to Ajit. He has a very specific criminal records which means those 26 victims were killed in a very similar and exact way. The very first of this kind of murder was when Ajit returned home from fishing and was covered in blood. While it turned out that, that was not the blood of fish.

This murder was of a woman called Advika Arora, and she was murdered the exact night that Ajit did not returned home. It is also the exact night he had come home covering in blood. Advika was found decapitated and her heart was cut out. Her body was found four plots away from Ajit's home. At the time the police had no idea who had done this murder, but now 16 years later, they now knew Ajit was responsible for this murder. The police also learned from Rishi that it was this murder of Advika that Roshni was concern about. With Rishi's testimony, and the way Advika was murdered, and where she was murdered, this was enough evidence for the police to close the case and definitely linked the murder of Advika to Ajit. But there was more murders. In 1996, the body of Adya Singh was found wrapped in a blanket on the side of a highway. She had also been decapitated and her heart cut out. Again, at the time the police had no idea who had killed her. Now, almost 9 years later, now the police knew Ajit criminal record, they reopened the case. Ajit kept meticulous records. He was a very organized person, which is probably how he was able to get away with all these murders.

He kept very meticulous records of all of the mileage that he did with his car. Moreover, on the day that Adya was murdered, Ajit has made an entry into his log that he kept, and he has done that amount of miles from his house to where Advika was found. However, not only that, a dark hair was found wrapped in a blanket where Advika was found. Amazingly, after searching Ajit's truck 9 years after the murder, dark hairs was also found in his truck. In addition, through DNA analysis, the dark hair found in Ajit's truck was an exact match with the dark hair found in the blanket where Advika's body were wrapped in. Again definitely linking another murder to Ajit. At this point, it is 100 percent confirmed that Ajit is a serial killer. He obviously murdered his mother, and now being discovered that he murdered two more women, we now know that he murdered his wife and his niece. In the beginning, he intended killing his entire family, but ended up killing his mother.

His father murdering his dog triggered all that. However, another big fact is that his big sister rejected him when he wanted to get married. Ishani was invited but she turned down the invitation because she does not want anything to do with him. In addition, this really hurt Ajit. Again, he felt like his sister abandoned him on the night he murdered his mother. It was the first murder that started it all, awakening the serial murder in him. The first and the last murder were so personal to Ajit. Roshni was a bubbling fun person, who loved her family and try to live life to the fullest. She put her trust in her husband Ajit, and he would tragically be the one to take her life. She stabbed in the heart by Ajit. She was only 38 years old. Saanvi was a loving caring person with a heart of gold. She loved spending time with friends and family. She loved her work as an accountant, and those she worked with. She loved the beach and many other things. Saanvi love the life and she was only 28 years old. Ajit's own mother, Diya, her life was taken away from her by her own son. And the many more victims Ajit had murdered. After the brutal murder of Roshni and Saanvi, Saanvi's mother and father petitioned for a new law to be passed that will allow the unveiling the juvenile records for those that have committed serious crimes, so that someone like Ajit would not be able to hide their murders and their past hidden from those close to them. They hoped that someday this law would be passed.

About the Author

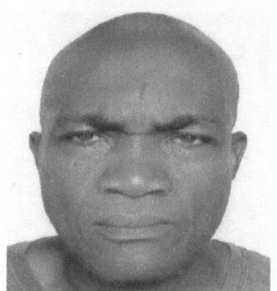

Bright Mills

Bright Mills is an IT Engineer, a historian, a writer and a publisher, from Nigeria. He started his writing career in 1999 when he was with the printing media. Mills loves writing despite his engineering career. He has written some interesting books of which one of them has to do with human trafficking.

www.ingramcontent.com/pod-product-compliance
Lightning Source LLC
LaVergne TN
LVHW041555070526
838199LV00046B/1974